# Operation Marriage

## Written by Cynthia Chin-Lee

## Illustrations by Lea Lyon

To the real Alex and Nikki, who inspired this, and to the
First Presbyterian Church of Palo Alto.
—C.C.

To my husband Bernie and all those
who are fighting for equality.
—L.L.

*Operation Marriage* © 2011 Cynthia Chin-Lee and Lea Lyon

This edition © 2011 Reach And Teach and PM Press
All rights reserved. No part of this book may be transmitted by
any means without permission in writing from the publisher.

PM Press
PO Box 23912
Oakland, CA 94623
www.pmpress.org

ISBN: 978-1-60486-422-9
Library of Congress Control Number: 2011927966

Interior layout by JBHR

Printed in Canada on recycled paper.

Reach And Teach
29 Mira Vista Court
Daly City, CA 94014
www.reachandteach.com

After school my best friend Zach said to me, "We can't be best friends anymore."

"Why not?"

"It's your parents, Alex. They're…they're not really married."

"Of course they're married," I said. My face got red hot.

"No, they're not. My dad says two women can't be married."

He dashed away.

I was so mad I felt like punching someone.

I got my little brother Nicky and we walked home.

When we arrived, I told Mama Kathy what happened.

She hugged me, but I didn't feel like hugging back.

Nicky told her. "We want you to get married to Mama Lee!"

"But Mama Lee and I are married," she said.

"But Zach's family doesn't think so," I said.

"You're right," Mama Kathy said. "We had a commitment ceremony, but we couldn't get a marriage license back then."

"So you're not really married?" I asked.

"Well, no, but we've done everything possible to have the same rights as married people. You know that I've adopted both of you."

Mama Lee came home from work and heard
what happened.

"Let's get out the videos."

She and Mama Kathy dug through the
trunks in the attic and got the video of their
commitment ceremony.

I giggled to see them so young
and pretty.

Nicky laughed at my
cousin Ryan, who
was a chubby ring
bearer.

"But it's not the same, Mom," I said. "People like Zach don't think you're married. Won't the state let you get married for real now?"

Mama Kathy said, "Yes, and we've tried for a long time to get that right. Now that we have it, other people are trying to take that away. But it's late now. Let's talk about it in the morning."

The next day as we got ready for school, Nicky said, "Are you going to get married?"

Mama Lee said, "Getting married is a lot of trouble."

Nicky frowned.

He whispered in my ear: "Operation Marriage."

After school, when we were supposed to be doing our homework, Nicky and I made plans.

"How about getting some wedding music and blasting it every morning?" I said.

"I know. We can make a wedding card for them," Nicky said.

"Or even better, a wedding program!"

Nicky and I made a fake wedding program like the one Joey's parents had at their wedding.

We got up the next morning and placed it on the kitchen table.

Mama Lee showed it to Mama Kathy right away. She smiled and said, "This wedding program is the best gift I've ever gotten."

Nicky said, "Well, when are you going to do it?"

Mama Lee said, "We have to think about it more."

The next day we heard news on the radio. Our parents looked worried. "Sounds like Prop 8 might pass. If it does, we won't be able to marry," Mama Kathy told us.

Soon, signs popped up in our neighborhood. Mama Lee hammered one into our lawn.

**Let's Keep California Great.**

**Vote No On Prop 8.**

I biked by Zach's house.

Zach's dad was putting a sign in their yard that said,

**Marriage Is For A Man and A Woman.**

I started to cry.

At dinner that night, I couldn't eat.

"What's wrong?" Mama Lee asked.

"You know Zach?" I said. "He was whispering something to Josh when I came into class, and they have a sign in the yard."

"Ouch. I'm so sorry, Alex," she said. "I saw the sign. I can't believe he stopped being your friend. His mom told me that he's confused."

Nicky piped up, "Mom, you hafta get married. For real!"

That weekend, Mama Kathy told us.

"Kids, we decided we're going to marry for real with a license and a church ceremony."

She pointed to me, "And you, Alex, will be a bridesmaid, and you, Nicky, will be the ring bearer."

We shopped for special clothes.

Nicky got a dark suit.

I got a lacey white dress and white
shoes to match.

Mama Kathy picked out
wedding flowers, and Mama
Lee baked yummy foods.

They said we could each
invite two friends.

I didn't invite Zach.

It was the happiest day of my life to see Pastor Rob marry our parents.

I read a poem that I wrote all by myself, and everyone cheered.

At school I showed the wedding photos to my friends. All of them were excited to see them.

Even Zach.

A month later, we were sad to hear that Prop 8 passed, but we were so glad our parents were married before that happened.

One day, the doorbell rang. Zach and his mother stood on our front porch with a plate of cookies. My mouth fell open in surprise.

"We're sorry," his mother said.

Zach added, "No matter what, I want to be your friend."

We invited them in.

Most kids don't get to see their parents marry. But we're not most kids.

In 2001, the Netherlands was the first country to recognize same-sex marriage. In addition, six other countries recognize same-sex marriage: Argentina, Belgium, Canada, Iceland, Norway, Portugal, South Africa, Spain, and Sweden.

In the United States, the states of Connecticut, Iowa, New York, Massachusetts, New Hampshire, and Vermont perform same-sex marriage. The state of California authorized same-sex marriage from June to November 2008, but this right was revoked when Proposition 8 passed. This law specified that marriage was only for a man and a woman. The state supreme court, however, upheld the approximately 18,000 same-sex marriages that took place in 2008. Two years later, a federal judge ruled that a ban against same-sex marriage is unconstitutional. Despite that ruling, at the time this book went to press, same-sex marriages are still not allowed in California, most of the United States, and most of the countries in the world.

This is based on the true story of my friends, the parents of Alex and Nikki, who married in October 2008 in Northern California.

# ABOUT PM PRESS

PM Press was founded at the end of 2007 by a small collection of folks with decades of publishing, media, and organizing experience. PM Press co-conspirators have published and distributed hundreds of books, pamphlets, CDs, and DVDs. Members of PM have founded enduring book fairs, spearheaded victorious tenant organizing campaigns, and worked closely with bookstores, academic conferences, and even rock bands to deliver political and challenging ideas to all walks of life. We're old enough to know what we're doing and young enough to know what's at stake.

We seek to create radical and stimulating fiction and non-fiction books, pamphlets, t-shirts, visual and audio materials to entertain, educate, and inspire you. We aim to distribute these through every available channel with every available technology—whether that means you are seeing anarchist classics at our bookfair stalls; reading our latest vegan cookbook at the café; downloading geeky fiction e-books; or digging new music and timely videos from our website.

PM Press
PO Box 23912
Oakland, CA 94623
www.pmpress.org

# ABOUT REACH AND TEACH

Reach And Teach is a peace and social justice learning company, transforming the world through teachable moments. They publish and distribute books, music, posters, games, curriculum, and DVDs that focus on peacemaking and healing the planet.

Reach And Teach
29 Mira Vista Court
Daly City, CA 94014
www.reachandteach.com